Circle the words that tell what is in the wagon.

bike   dog   ball   car

cat   book   clown   train

Draw a line from each word to the picture that goes with it.

who

he

they

it

she

Circle the word that goes with each picture.

dig   dad   dog

pig   dig   pat

big   bug   bad

cut   cap   cat

Draw a line from each word
to the picture that goes with it.

three

one

two

six

four

Color each ball.

brown

black

blue

red

green

yellow

5

The letters are mixed up.
Put the letters together to spell a word.
Write the word in the spaces.

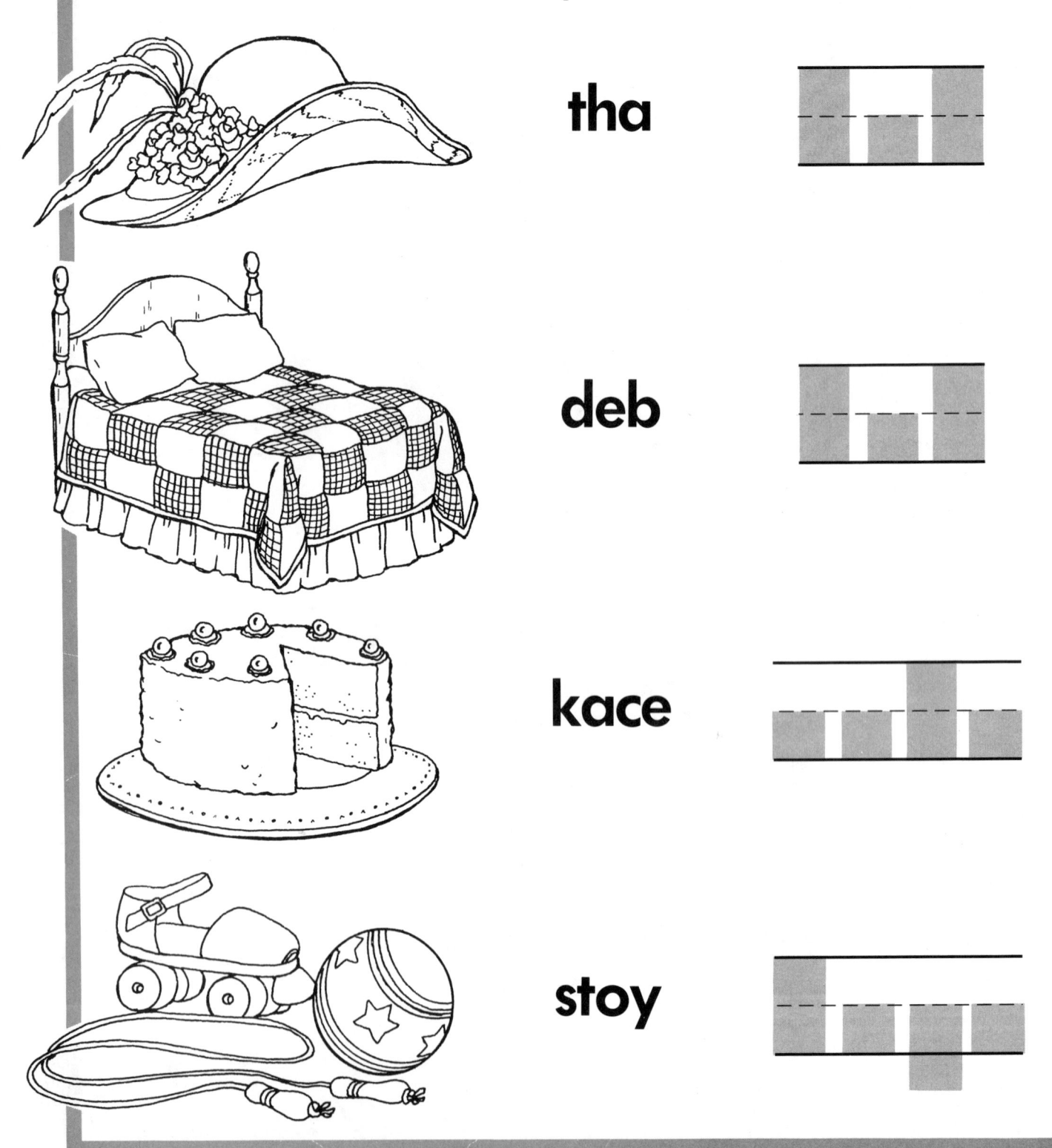

tha

deb

kace

stoy

Circle the word that goes with each picture.

walk   ride   run

eat   drink   sleep

eat   make   walk

ride   take   see

Circle the words that tell what is on the wagon.

cat   frog   sheep   bat

pen   beep   hen   cake

**Start at one.
Connect the dots.
Color the picture.**

seven

eight

six

nine
ten
eleven
three
twelve
five
two
four one

Draw a line from each sentence to the picture that goes with it.

I ride a bike.

I see a bike.

He makes a cake.

He eats a cake.

The letters are mixed up.
Put the letters together to spell a word.
Write the word in the spaces.

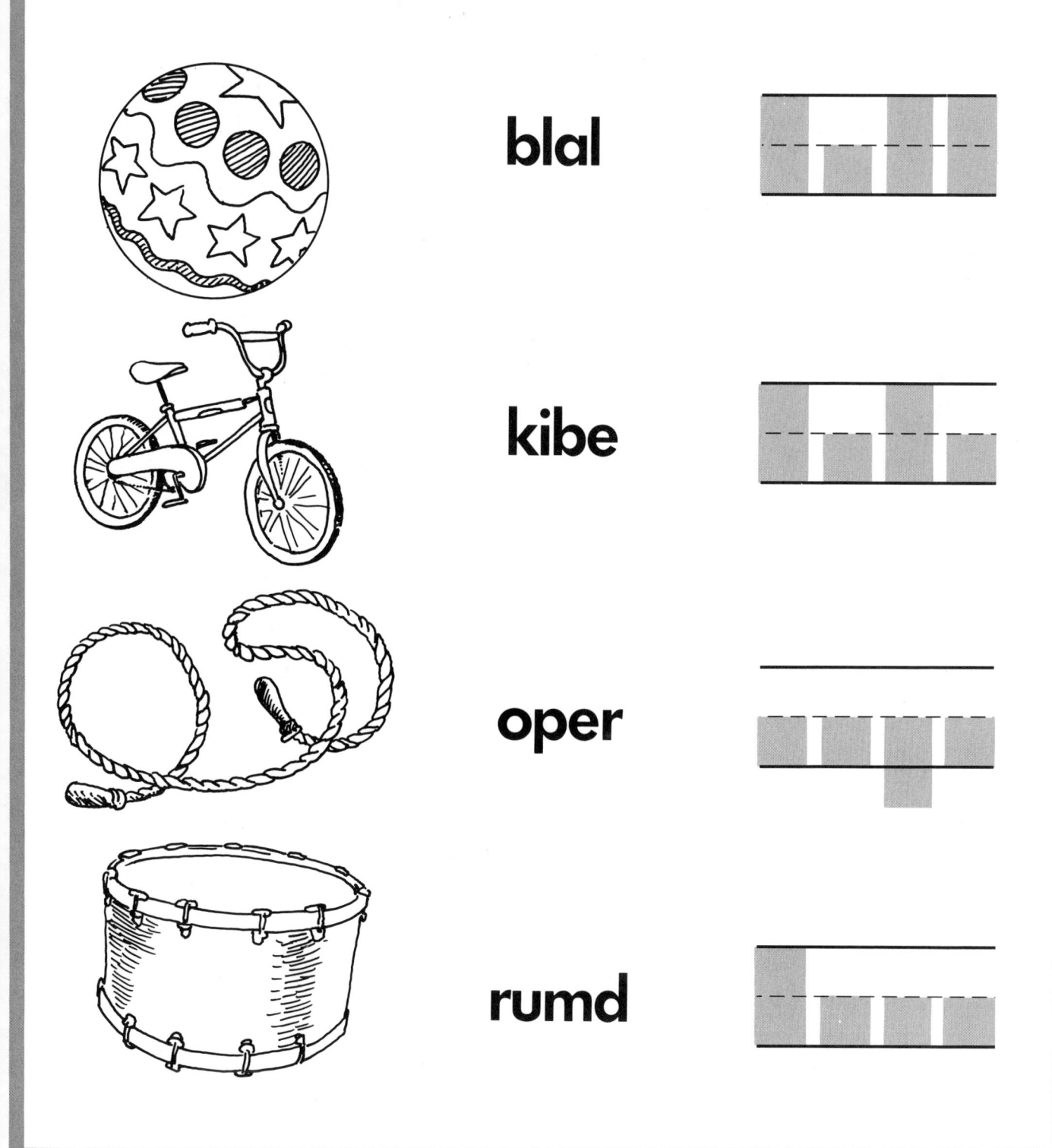

blal

kibe

oper

rumd

Draw a line from each picture to the word that goes with it.

fly

run

walk

sit

sleep

Draw a line from each picture to the word that goes with it.

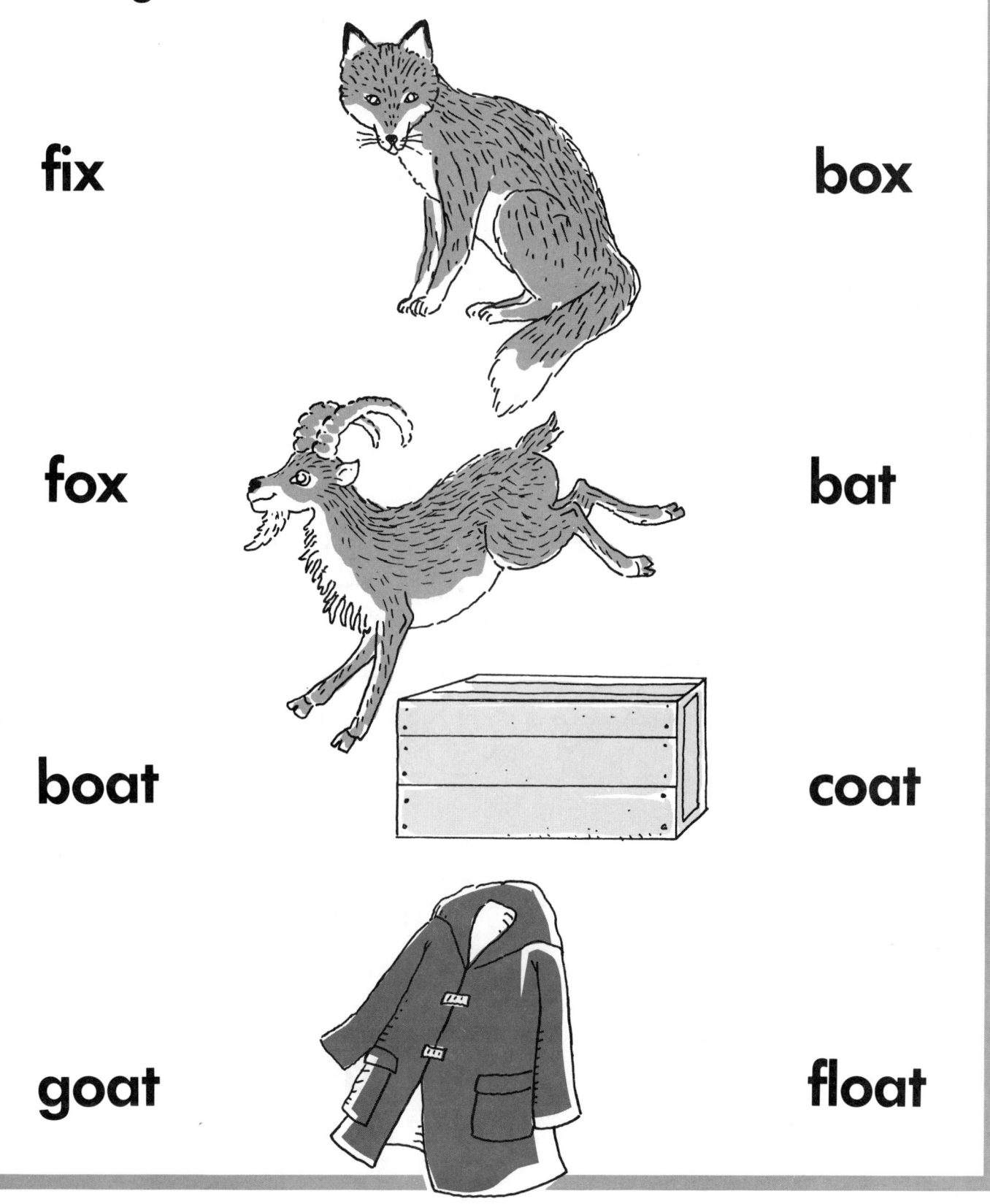

fix　　　　　　　　　　　　　　　　　　box

fox　　　　　　　　　　　　　　　　　　bat

boat　　　　　　　　　　　　　　　　　coat

goat　　　　　　　　　　　　　　　　　float

Circle the words that name animals.

bear	toys	mouse	goose
horse	elephant	wagon	house

Circle the picture that goes with each sentence.

One frog ran.

She can fly.

Six cats sat.

He eats the cake.

Read the words.
Draw a line from each set of words
to the picture that goes with it.
Then color the pictures.

red car **blue hat** **brown bear**

lack sheep	yellow coat	green frog

Draw a line from each word to the number that goes with it.

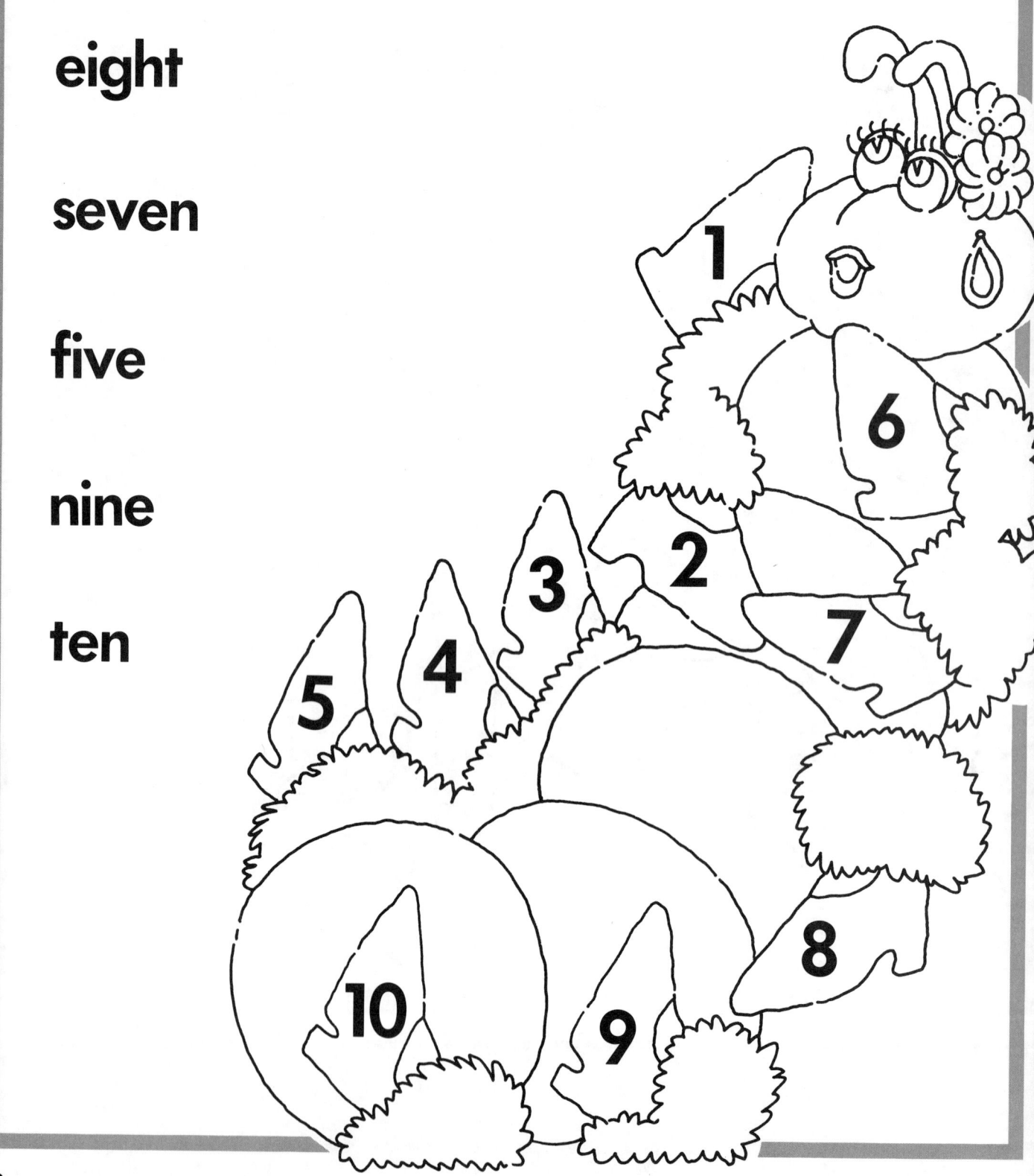

eight

seven

five

nine

ten

Circle the picture that goes with each word.

cold

small

big

hot

19

Circle the words that tell what is in the wagon.

| hat | pig | mouse | baby |
| elephant | drum | goose | clown |

20

Circle the word that goes with the shaded picture.

tall   **short**

sad   **happy**

good   **bad**

slow   **fast**

Draw a line from each set of words to the picture that goes with it.

one foot

some feet

all of the feet

no feet

Draw a line from each set of words to the picture that goes with it.

to the house

from the house

up the stairs

down the stairs

before the bear

after the bear

23

Circle the words that name toys.

| doll | elephant | tree | kite |
| mouse | ball | bear | blocks |

24

Draw a line from each word
to the picture that goes with it.

fall

pull

hold

buy

jump

25

Circle the word that goes with each picture.

funny   sad   long

long   old   pretty

old   cold   sad

tall   sad   long

Draw a line from each word to the picture that goes with it.

under

over

in

out

on

off

27

Circle the word that goes with the shaded picture.

big   bigger   biggest

cold   colder   coldest

small   smaller   smallest

hot   hotter   hottest

Draw a line from each sentence to the picture that goes with it.

This boy is happy.

That boy is sad.

Pull the wagon.

Hold the rope.

Read the words.
Draw a line from each set of words
to the picture that goes with it.
Then color the pictures.

new yellow hat

cold orange cat

hot black cat

old green hat

Circle the picture that goes with each sentence.

The cat is in the wagon.

The cat ran under the wagon.

The cat ran after the dog.

The cat is on the box.

31

Make one word out of two words.
Draw a line between the two words
that make one new word.

hair	coat
bird	ball
foot	brush
rain	bath